Countdown

A Good with Numbers I

By
Rose Bak

ROSE BAK

COUNTDOWN TO LOVE
© 2019 by Rose Bak
Second edition © 2020 by Rose Bak

About This Book

Holly has given up on dating, but the hot new guy at the office has his eye on her. The only problem is that he's way too young for her. Nate can't possibly be interested in a curvy 45-year-old when he can have his pick of women half her age. Or can he?

The minute Nate lays eyes on Holly he is done. Done dating. Done playing around. Done looking. He's finally found the one – he just needs to convince her that he's serious about her and that their age difference doesn't matter. As they count down to the end of the year, can Nate convince Holly to make loving him her New Year's resolution?

"Countdown to Love" is the fourth book in the Good with Numbers holiday novella series. This steamy standalone workplace romance is a fun short read featuring a seasoned independent woman, a cocky younger man, meddling friends, and a holiday HEA.

This book includes a special except from "Until You Came Along", book one of the Oliver Boys Band series, available now from select retailers.

Be sure to join Rose's mailing list and get a free book. Click here[1] to be the first to hear about all the latest releases and special sales.

---

1.   https://bit.ly/rosebaknews

Holly

"Have you tried online dating?"

I moved my forehead down towards the conference table and slowly began hitting my head against the shiny wood surface.

"What?" my friend and coworker Lana asked. "I have heard that a lot of people find great relationships that way."

I stopped my slow pounding to ask, "Do you actually personally know anyone who has found a good relationship through online dating?"

"Well, no," Lana admitted grudgingly. "But I'm sure people have. You hear it all the time."

I raised my head and gave her a hard look.

"Let me tell you about online dating. Every guy from age 25 to 60 is looking for a skinny young 25-year-old. It's in almost every profile. Sometimes it's coded language like 'must be fit and energetic' and sometimes they're all out there like 'must be under 30, no fatties allowed'. Never mind if they themselves are balding with a stomach like Santa Claus."

Lana laughed. "Come on Holly, it can't be that bad."

"Oh but it is," I answered. "Occasionally you'll find one who will talk to you, but they just want a fast hook-up and expect you to be pathetically grateful that they were willing to give a pity fuck to a chunky middle-aged woman."

"You are NOT chunky," Lana protested. "And you're 44, not 60."

"I'm 45," I corrected. "I'll be 50 soon and it will all be over for me. I have decided to cut my losses. I'm giving up on dating for good. It's just not worth the trouble when I have a perfectly good battery-operated boyfriend in the drawer."

Lana snorted. "You'll find someone Holly, I'll help you," she said. "Ian has some single friends our age that you might like."

"See this is the problem with people in love," I retorted. "You were all 'dating sucks' until you fell in love with Ian. Now you have a weird obsession with pairing off everyone else to be in a relationship like you."

"I'm just saying, don't give up yet. It will happen for you," Lana answered, with the smug self-assuredness of someone happily in love.

I shook my head at her as James, our boss, came in to start our weekly management team meeting. "Yeah OK, Lana, whatever you say."

I turned my attention to James. We had known each other since we were kids, but I had just started working for him a few years ago. We had run into each other right after I was downsized from the tech company I had been working for, and he offered me a job on the spot.

I was technically only his assistant, but I was also his confidante and go-to for special projects. I was way overqualified for the job, but James paid me well and it was low stress, which worked out great for me. I loved having time and energy after work to do other things that interested me, like volunteering and yoga and crafting. I never had time for that when I worked 70-hour weeks at the tech company.

"Good morning everyone," James started, as I took out my notepad to jot down the highlights of the meeting. "First up on our agenda, our new public relations and marketing person started this morning. As you know, adding this new position came out of the recommendations that Ian and his group made."

Ian was Lana's fiancé. They had met here at the office when he came in as a consultant to overhaul our media platforms and create a marketing program to help us grow our business more planfully. After working with us for almost a year, Ian had determined that we were finally in a place to do it ourselves. The new guy was brought in to create an in-house team focusing on public relations, marketing, and social media.

There was a knock on the door and a man stepped in. "Ah, Nate, right on time. Done with HR I see," James said jovially. "Come in and meet the team. Everyone, this is our new marketing director, Nathanial

Bowerman. Nate comes to us from the communications team at Regency Hotels."

The new guy eased into an open seat across the table from me and threw out a friendly smile to the group. "Good morning everyone, as James said, my name is Nate. I'm thrilled to be here and am looking forward to working with all of you."

Nate turned his head in my direction, giving me a casual nod, and I caught my breath.

He looked young, maybe 30, and he was beautiful. There was no other word for it. He had dark brown curly hair and chocolate brown eyes framed by lashes so ridiculously long I could see them from several feet away. High cheek bones and a square chin with an adorable cleft in it. He was tall and lean but clearly with some good muscles, as evidenced by his biceps that were stretching against the sleeves of his shirt.

Yum. Such a cute boy. He looked like an older version of Gilbert Blythe from the 1980s version of Anne of Green Gables.

James asked us to go around the room and introduce ourselves and when we got to me, Nate met my eyes. For a moment everything in the room seemed to still and fade away. My heart started racing like I was going to have a heart attack. His gaze was warm and friendly yet there was something there, something that made me feel drawn to him.

Get a grip Holly, I admonished myself.

Nate seemed startled, like maybe he felt something between us as well. His eyes flared in interest as he studied me for longer than was polite.

Lana cleared her throat next to me and I realized that Nate and I were just sitting there staring at each other silently instead of me introducing myself as expected.

"Hi Nate, I'm Holly," I finally found my voice. "Executive assistant for James."

Nate smiled and his entire face lit up. I felt my panties dampen even as I chastised myself for lusting after the youngster. He was clearly a charmer. "Such a pleasure to meet you Holly," he said, his voice deep and warm.

We finished introductions then moved through several agenda items until we came to the last one on the list: the annual holiday party for clients which was scheduled for the first weekend in December. The event was a huge deal that people flew in from around the country to attend. There were optional activities the day after the party for clients who wanted to make a weekend out of it.

"We will be using the same event planner as we have the past three years," James said. "And Holly, as usual I would like you to be their liaison and lead from our team. We all appreciated the excellent work you have done in the past on making the event memorable."

I nodded, feeling a rush of gratitude at his praise. My last boss never had a kind word for anyone. "Of course James, I'm glad to do it."

James continued. "And Nate, you will work with Holly to handle the PR and marketing of the event. We will look forward to seeing what you come up with."

Nate nodded as James continued, "You and Holly will have to work closely to make sure this is the best event ever."

"Sure thing James," Nate said. He looked over at me and added, "I'm looking forward to it."

I felt a little thrill run down my spine at his words, which was ridiculous. He was just being polite.

The meeting finally ended, and I gathered up my coffee cup and notebook, walking out with Lana.

"Holly!" I heard someone call behind me. I turned to see Nate walking up to me, his gait smooth and confident. I looked up at him, my gaze fixated on the dimple in his chin. He was at least six inches taller than me.

"Can I help you?" I asked formally.

Nate nodded. "When should we get together to chat about the event?" he asked. "I would like to get up to speed as soon as possible."

"I'll send you an appointment," I responded, feeling unreasonably annoyed even though his request was completely reasonable. "In the meantime, I will send you some information to look at from previous events so you can see what we have done with them. Just let me know if you need anything."

Nate

"Let me know if you need anything," Holly said, turning to leave the conference room.

How about you, under me, screaming my name, I thought to myself.

I watched her walk away with Ian's fiancée, her rear curvy and luscious in the fitted skirt she wore. Holly was adorable. She had dark curly hair with golden-toned highlights, olive skin that hinted of some Hispanic or Native heritage, and large expressive dark eyes. She was probably six inches shorter than my 6 feet, the perfect size for me to tuck her under my chin.

When our eyes met across the table at the meeting today, I knew I was done.

After 36 years I had finally found the woman I was looking for. It was like I was struck by lightning and my soul called out, "She's the one." Of course I would have to trade in my man card if I said that out loud. I could not believe I was even thinking this way about someone I just met, and yet it felt right.

I came from a long line of people who had fallen in love at first sight. My father and grandfather always told me stories about how they had known that they had met the woman they would marry when they first laid eyes on them. I had never been totally sure I believed it. Until today.

I knew that taking this new position would be life changing, but I had no idea how much. I could not wait to get to know Holly better.

I went through my first day doing all the typical things: setting up my email, figuring out where to get office supplies, meeting my coworkers, finding the men's room. The hours flew by, but those dark eyes of Holly's kept haunting me whenever I paused. I kept hoping for another glimpse of her, but our paths did not cross again for the rest of the day.

I was glad we had been assigned to work together, it would give me an excuse to get to know her. She said she would send me an appointment to get involved in planning the event and I was already looking forward to it. It was the first time in my career that I was eager to add another meeting to my schedule.

At the end of the day I came around the corner on my way to the elevator. The doors were just closing so I jumped in quickly, already having learned that the elevators in this building were incredibly slow. I heard a small intake of breath and realized my day was looking up. Holly was the sole occupant of the elevator car.

I turned and gave her my most charming smile, moving to stand closer to her than strictly professional. I could feel Holly's nearness vibrating through my body even as she studiously studied the buttons on the elevator panel as if she were riding with a total stranger.

"Hello Holly, how was your day?"

She blinked a few times before answering. "Oh. Um. Fine," she stuttered adorably. From this angle I could see a pulse beating furiously in her neck. I was making her nervous. Good, she was off balance too, just like me. "How was your first day?"

I edged a tiny bit closer to her and she started to step back before she caught herself. Holly straightened up to her full height, her back ramrod straight.

"Great," I said, meeting her deep brown eyes. "It would be even better if you would have dinner with me."

Her eyes widened in surprise. "What?"

"Dinner," I answered with my most charming smile. "It's the meal people usually have around this time every day. We can get to know each other better."

She shot me an annoyed look as if my forwardness irritated her. "No thanks."

"A drink then?" I pressed.

"No," she shot back quickly.

"Do you have other plans?" I asked.

I could see her thinking about lying before she said, "No. But I've had a long day. I appreciate the offer, but I don't usually go out with people I don't know."

"You've never been on a blind date?" I asked her incredulously.

"Of course I have," she answered, her brow wrinkled in confusion. "I've had many blind dates."

I raised my eyebrows and she continued. "I mean, I know you aren't asking me on a date, my point was we just met today, and it would be a little awkward and...."

"But I was asking you on a date," I interrupted her.

Her forehead scrunched for a second then she glared at me. "Haha Gilbert. Good one. Didn't anyone tell you it's not nice to make fun of your elders?"

"It's Nate," I reminded her.

"I know," she shot back as the elevator doors opened. She hurried out into the parking garage. I followed her as she damn near sprinted out into the garage, her heels pounding against the cement floor as she moved.

"So, is that a 'no' on dinner then?" I called out to her quickly retreating back.

"Goodnight," she called over her shoulder, ignoring my question as she race-walked towards her car. "See you at work tomorrow."

I smiled to myself as I watched to make sure Holly got into her car safely, then walked to my own car. The Holly I had seen at work today was cool and confident, nothing like the flustered woman racing away from me. She felt something. I was sure of it. I just needed to give her time and not come on too strong.

Normally it wasn't in my nature to be pushy anyway, but something about being around Holly made me want to stake my claim and lock her down before some other guy got there. It made no sense, especially since we had known each other for less than twelve hours, and yet there it was.

As soon as I got home, I shed my clothes and went right to the shower. I had been half hard since I first laid eyes on Holly that morning and standing in the elevator, smelling her sweet scent, my cock had hardened and pressed painfully against my pants. I needed some relief.

I closed my eyes and leaned against the tiled wall, my hand gripping my cock and moving up and down quickly. I imagined that Holly was in the shower with me, that wild hair everywhere as she kneeled before me, taking me in that stern little mouth of hers. My hand quickened as I imagined my cock gliding in and out of her mouth while she watched me with those dark serious eyes. I came on my hand with a loud groan.

This job is going to be interesting, I thought to myself as I dried off with a towel.

***

The next morning, I exited the elevator with two steaming cups, and headed towards the office next to James. I had scoped out the area the day before and noticed Holly's name on the door, so I knew where to find her.

"Knock knock," I called cheerfully as I stepped into her office.

I looked around, noting that everything was clean and neatly organized. Holly was at her desk, frowning at the computer with a pen between her teeth. Even though it was a few minutes before 9:00 she had clearly been here for a while already.

"Just a minute," she said distractedly. She got the most adorable line between her eyebrows as she stared in concentration at the monitor.

I took advantage of her distracted state to run my eyes over the parts of her body visible behind the desk. She wore a form-fitting green sweater that clung to her generous curves, and several bracelets stacked on one arm. Her hair was pulled into some kind of twist, but several tendrils of her hair had already escaped to frame her heart shaped face. She was lovely.

Holly sighed, pressed a button on her computer then turned her chair around to face me. "Oh," she said with a start when she saw me, as if surprised it was me and not someone else. "Good morning Nate. How can I help you?"

I moved across her office to stand in front of her and placed a coffee on the desk. She craned her neck up to look at me curiously. "I brought you caffeine," I said.

She looked confused. "Oh. Thanks. That's very nice of you but I don't drink coffee," she said a little dismissively.

"Coconut milk chai latte," I said, sliding it closer to her with my sexiest smile.

Her eyes widened as she looked at the drink then back up at me. "H-how did you know that?"

"I asked the barista in the lobby what your favorite drink was," I answered. "I noticed they seem to know everyone in the building by name, as well as their preferred drinks. I asked and it turns out that they knew yours too."

She grabbed the cup and took a small sip, softly sighing and closing her eyes in pleasure. I immediately felt tightening in my pants. Is that how she looked when she came? I couldn't wait to find out. I willed my dick to stay down. I wasn't going to make a good impression on all my new coworkers if I sported a perpetual hard-on like a teenaged boy.

"It's perfect," she said, taking another sip from the white paper cup. She gifted me with a sweet smile and my heart pounded painfully in my chest. She was so beautiful. "Thanks the chai, I hadn't gotten down there yet to get some."

"No problem," I said, walking backwards towards the door.

She looked confused by my departure like maybe she expected me to linger a while, but I was playing the long game. I knew she needed some time to get used to me, and I didn't want to spook her. Plus, this job was important to me. It was a big step in my career taking this promotion, and I did not want to get a reputation as being a slacker.

"Have a great day," I called as I stepped back out into the hallway. "Let me know when you want to get together to get me up to speed on the customer appreciation event."

An email came from Holly a few hours later. *Nate, I just got off the phone with the event planner, can you join us for a meeting today at 2:00 in the main conference room? I'm attaching some information for you to review.*

I quickly wrote back confirming my availability and added it to my calendar. I couldn't wait to see her again, even if it was for a meeting.

I spent the next few hours writing a press release and looking over the information Holly had sent. It was thorough and organized including room schematics, timelines, invitation lists and an exceptionally detailed "to do" list for every week leading up to the event.

My calendar reminder beeped and I realized it was already 2:00 pm. I had been so engrossed in my work that I lost track of time. My stomach growled as I walked towards the conference room, reminding me I had not gotten lunch yet. Oh well, too late to stop and get something now.

Holly sat on one side of the table with another woman sitting at the head of the table next to her. I saw now that Holly's form-fitting sweater was paired with another one of those sexy pencil skirts. My eyes skirted to her long legs, crossed at the knees, and her kitten heels.

"Nate, this is Jessica, our event planner. Jessica, Nate Bowerman, our new PR person."

Jessica rose to shake my hand, her eyes shining with interest. She was probably around my age, tall and thin and impeccably groomed, from her dyed blonde hair to her designer label dress. She held onto my hand a moment longer than necessary, maintaining eye contact as she smiled. I saw the interest in her eyes but unfortunately, she did nothing for me.

Holly cleared her throat, drawing Jessica's attention back to her. "Shall we get started?" Holly asked, her tone frosty as her eyes bounced between us. Interesting.

We went through the details of the event, each of us taking notes as we divvied up the assignments. Jessica was super efficient, completing the meeting in under an hour. I was glad to be finished since she kept looking at me like she was stranded in the desert and I was a glass of water. Jessica stood to leave, shaking first Holly's hand, then mine, once again giving me meaningful eye contact which I ignored.

"I'll email you both the project chart by tomorrow," she promised. Her voice lowered to a sultry tone. "I'm really going to look forward to working with you, Nate."

I nodded then grimaced as my stomach rumbled loudly. "Sorry about that," I laughed as we all walked out of the room together, "I haven't gotten around to finding lunch yet."

I ambled back to my office and was about to sit down when I heard a knock. Holly. I looked up with a surprised smile. "Holly! Hi."

She walked in, purpose in her stride, and placed a paper bag on my desk. I looked at it in confusion then looked back at her. "The other half of my turkey sandwich," she said, not meeting my gaze. "And there's an apple and a bag of chips in there too. Eat."

Her cheeks turned pink, as if she were embarrassed. "Don't skip lunch, Gilbert, it's not good for you."

She turned on her heel and rushed out while I watched her go. *I knew it,* I thought to myself. *She likes me.*

Holly

"Caffeine?"

I looked up to see Nate moving towards my desk. It was Monday morning and for the fifth consecutive day he was bringing me a chai latte, prepared just the way I liked it. I had stopped visiting the coffee cart in the morning because he was bringing me my drink every morning anyway.

"Thanks, but you really shouldn't bring me chai every day," I said, repeating what I had said to him the last four times he had brought me the beverage.

"I don't mind," he replied, just as he had the last four days. He slid the drink across my desk and plopped down in one of the visitor chairs. This was new. The last four days he had dropped off my chai and left without a word, like some kind of tea hit-and-run.

"So how was your weekend Holly?" he asked with what could only be described as a panty-dropping smile. "Did you miss me?"

In addition to the daily chai drop-offs, somehow we had managed to run into each other several times every day last week...in the copy room, the elevator, the employee lounge, even in the hallway between the restrooms. If I didn't know better, I would think he was turning up on purpose to see me.

Sure, we worked on the same floor, but I could go an entire week without seeing most of the people who worked on this floor. Whenever he saw me, Nate was super flirty and charming. And he always seemed to be standing too close, like he had no concept of personal space. It was starting to piss me off.

I told myself for at least the tenth time that I should not have brought him that sandwich last week. It seemed to have encouraged him in some way. I couldn't explain why I had fed him like that. For some reason, knowing he was hungry had just brought out the nurturer in me. At least for a few minutes.

I did not believe for a minute that Nate was actually interested in me, not when he could be with someone his own age like Jessica, the event planner who had been openly flirting with him during the meeting last week. Yet he hadn't seemed attracted to Jessica, despite her obvious interest. I was the one he focused his flirting on.

Was I some kind of challenge to him? A diversion? It didn't make sense.

I wagged my finger at him. "Stop flirting with me Gilbert," I ordered. "It's not appropriate."

"You're not wearing a ring," he pointed out affably, nodding towards my empty left hand. That was another thing that was pissing me off about him, no matter how rude I was to him, he seemed unfazed by it. Or amused.

He smiled at me indulgently. "I know you're not dating anyone, and neither am I, so why is it inappropriate to flirt with you?"

"Because we're coworkers," I said sternly. "How do you know I'm not dating anyone?"

"I asked Ian, and he asked Lana," he said, smirking.

"Lana!" I muttered under my breath. She had brought up Nate several times in the past week, insisting she had noticed an attraction between us and encouraging me to pursue him.

"Besides, us being coworkers isn't a problem," he continued. "There's no policy against it. I know Lana and Ian met here at work. Lana told me her friend Maya is with Anthony who used to be her boss, and that James met his fiancée here at work too, so I'm pretty sure no one will say anything about us dating. Come to dinner with me tonight Holly."

"We're not going to be dating," I answered quickly and firmly, even as my heart quickened at the idea. Jesus, maybe Lana was right, I needed to make more of an effort to start dating again. Not him of course, although my greedy body was begging me to climb him like a tree. He was so tall and strong and handsome.

And young Holly, I reminded myself sternly. *Don't forget he's too young for you.*

"Why can't we date?" he asked, leaning forward in his chair and resting his elbows on my desk. I tried not to notice his strongly corded forearms, covered with dark hair. "We're both single. There's an obvious attraction between us, I can see it in your eyes. I wouldn't be pursuing you if I didn't think this was mutual."

I sighed. He was right, not that I would admit that. Ever since he started working here, I had caught myself staring at him, fantasizing about him, dreaming of him. It wasn't like me to daydream about a boy.

"That doesn't matter, Gilbert, it's just not going to happen."

He frowned. "What's with the Gilbert thing?"

I leaned forward, matching his posture. "You remind me of Gilbert Blythe," I said, nodding towards him. "The curly brown hair, the chin, the eyes...."

"Who's Gilbert Blythe?" he asked in confusion.

"He's a character in a movie called Anne of Green Gables," I answered with a deep sigh. "Which brings me to your other question. Not only do I not date coworkers, but you are way too young for me. Go hit on someone your own age."

"What are you talking about?" he asked. "Age doesn't matter. We are both adults. It's not like I'm your high school intern or something."

"Are you even thirty yet?" I asked him curiously. I had been dying to find out his age to see how much of an age difference there was. Not that I cared, of course.

He drew himself up to sit up straight. "I'm 36, so I haven't been under 30 for quite a while," he said.

I made a "you see?" gesture with my hand and he continued with a small frown. "Why, how old are you?"

"I'm 45," I answered archly. "I could practically be your mother."

"Nine-year-olds don't usually have babies Holly," he answered. "Age is just a number. Sure, a nine year difference would have been a lot when we were kids, but at this age, it doesn't matter much."

"You do not want to be dating a middle-aged woman," I told him firmly. "Now run along, it's almost time for the Monday morning leadership team meeting."

He leaned forward again, reaching across the desk and tucking a strand of hair behind my ear before he brought his large warm hand to my cheek. I sat frozen in my seat. I resisted the urge to rub my cheek against him like my body was begging me to do. I could feel the heat of his hand seeping through my face, warming me up, making my whole body hum.

Holding my breath, I was trembling with the effort of keeping myself still. This close I could smell his cologne and see the amber flecks in his warm brown eyes.

"You know what I think Holly?" he said softly. "I think you feel the same strong attraction that I feel, and it scares you, so you're using work and our age difference as an excuse to protect yourself."

I pulled away from his hand and stood up quickly, drawing my spine straight and giving him a glare. The nerve of him. *He's not wrong,* my pesky conscience reminded me.

"The only thing I feel is the need to get to our meeting on time," I told him icily. "Go find someone your own age to play with, Gilbert."

I grabbed my chai and notepad and hurried out of my office. Nate of course fell in step right next to me. I studiously ignored him as we headed down the long corridor to the meeting room.

We walked in together and I moved towards an open spot next to Lana. Nate slid into the seat on my other side. He placed his hand on the chair behind me, his fingers brushing my back as he leaned in and whispered into my ear, "I think you protest too much Holly."

19

I shivered as he moved back to his own space. I could sense Lana looking at me questioningly, but I ignored her as James started the meeting.

An hour later I was doodling as our CFO droned on about the company budget and revenue forecasts. As a group, accountants were not the most exciting presenters, but this guy gave new meaning to the word 'boring'. James said he was excellent at his work though.

"Our projections are showing that if we continue at this same rate of growth, our client base will increase 20% over the next three years..."

I let out a small gasp as I felt something on my leg. I looked down to see Nate's hand resting on the bare skin of my thigh, just above the knee. He started drawing tiny circles there with one long finger, while keeping his gaze on the CFO as if nothing was happening.

I looked around but no one was paying us any attention. The lights were off in the room so we could see the PowerPoint, and everyone was looking at the presentation and apparently lulled into a bored stupor. Even James seemed to be having a hard time staying awake.

I moved my hand down and placed it on top of Nate's, intending to push him off, but he turned his hand up and captured my fingers so we were holding hands. I tried to subtly pull my hand away, but he held my hand still, rubbing the pad of his thumb across the skin on the inside of my wrist. His finger felt rough against my soft skin and I idly wondered what he did in his free time to build up callouses on his hands.

My pulse was beating rapidly, and I knew he must feel it too. I tried not to notice how good it felt to hold his hand but sweet baby Jesus, it felt good. A strong current of electricity seemed to move between our hands and up my body. I could feel my entire body flushing with arousal as our joined hands rested on the bare skin of my thigh. I suddenly wished I had chosen pants instead of a skirt today, at least I would have some kind of barrier between us.

I squeezed my legs together to ease the ache between them and Nate shot me a knowing look before returning his attention to the presentation. It felt so wrong, and yet so right. I sat there stiffly, all of my attention focused on our joined hands and the energy pulsing between us. My breath was coming in small rapid spurts and I was actively trying not to moan – or throw myself into Nate's lap. In the back of my mind I was embarrassed by my reaction. This was so wrong. Why wasn't I pulling away?

When the lights came on Nate finally let go of my hand, bringing his own hand back onto the tabletop. His hand clenched into a fist as if, like me, he was trying to control himself. He looked over at me and winked and I felt a jolt through my core. I was so screwed.

Nate

The rest of my Monday flew by. I was in back-to-back meetings most of the day, and it was after 5:00 before I knew it. I was just reaching to turn off my computer when I heard my door close. I looked up and saw Holly standing in front of it, her expression 100% pissed off female.

"Hi Hol," I said casually. "How's it going?"

"What the hell was that today?" she asked angrily.

"What are you talking about?" I asked innocently, walking over to stand in front of her.

She gritted her teeth and I swear I could see smoke coming out of her ears. Clearly she had been fuming about this all afternoon.

"This morning," she gritted out. "In the team meeting. You touched my leg and held my hand. What the fuck."

I nodded and gave her a small satisfied smile. "Oh yeah, that was fun, huh?"

Despite my cocky attitude I was shocked by my own behavior this morning. I had never, and I mean never, crossed a line at work like that. It was like I was outside my body watching myself grab her hand and I had been powerless to resist.

"What the – no it was NOT fun," she retorted, practically sputtering with anger. "What is WRONG with you?"

"Are you saying you didn't enjoy it?" I said moving closer. Her eyes widened and I could see the excitement flaring in them. My cock perked up in response and all my attention was laser focused on her face. I knew I was coming on a bit strong but somehow it seemed like the right approach, so I just went with my instincts.

Her pupils were dilated, and I could see the pulse in her throat beating like crazy. My own heart rate increased to match hers, as if our bodies where totally in sync. All other sound faded away except for our rough breathing.

22

"No, I did not enjoy it," she protested weakly, almost as if she were trying to convince herself as well as me. "It was totally inappropriate. What would people think if they had seen us?"

"They probably would have thought we are hot for each other," I answered. "Because we are."

I stepped closer and she took a half a step back until her back hit the closed door behind her. I crowded into her space until we were an inch apart. "You seemed to enjoy it," I argued. "I could practically smell your panties getting wet for me as your pulse raced underneath my fingers. You kept shifting in your chair like you were trying to get yourself off."

"You have a lot of fucking nerve," she gasped in shock.

"Are you denying that your panties were wet for me this morning?" I asked softly. I placed my hands on the door on either side of her head, crowding her, but I still didn't touch her.

"Are you denying that you're attracted to me? That you've been thinking of me? Because I've been thinking of you non-stop since we met, Holly."

Her breath hitched and I saw a brief flare of panic in her eyes as a pink blush crept up her face. That blush told me everything I needed to know.

"In fact, I bet if I touched you I would find out that your panties are wet right now," I kept on, bringing my lips close to hers, almost touching. "I bet you are wondering when I'm going to kiss you, hoping for it. Knowing that once we kiss, it will change everything."

She slid her hands up between us and pushed on my chest. "Back off Gilbert," she said sharply, her breath coming out in short pants. "Get out of my space."

I took a step back and brought my hands down to my sides, palms out placatingly. "It's OK Holly, I can see you're not ready yet," I said softly. "I can be patient. I can wait for you. But know this, when we do kiss, it will be because you initiate it. I guarantee it will change your life. And mine."

She sputtered. "Oh my god you're delusional," she said. "I'm not going to kiss you. I'm not going to date you. Go find a woman your own damn age." She turned towards the door and threw over her shoulder, "And keep your damn hands to yourself."

She grabbed the door handle and pulled it open, storming off without another word. I dropped into the closest chair, feeling drained from the encounter. She was running scared now. I took a risk pushing her, and it may have backfired on me.

I dialed my behavior back after that. I had to admit that Holly was right, I had been inappropriate, touching her in the meeting. I had been coming on too strong, too fast and I couldn't blame her for freaking out.

I still brought her chai every morning but limited our conversation to polite chit chat. We had our weekly meeting with the event planner, and I kept everything professional. Well, mostly professional. I had to confess that every time we were together, even if we passed in the hallway, I couldn't resist standing a little closer than strictly necessary. It was like I was a magnet and she was steel, my body just gravitated towards her without any effort from me. . I was fascinated by her scent, the way her cheeks flushed when I got too close, the way her eyes begged me to kiss her even while her face told me to back off.

The rest of the week flew by, busy but uneventful. I sat across from her at the next Monday leadership meeting, wanting to avoid the temptation of touching her. I looked up at one point to find Holly staring at me. She met my eyes, and a dark flush colored her face as she realized she'd been busted. The corner of my mouth quirked up into a smile as we stared at each other, neither of us moving.

"Holly. Nate." James brought our attention back to the meeting and we both started before turning to face his direction. "Can we get an update on the client appreciation party please?"

Holly cleared her throat. "Um, yes," she started slowly, clearly a bit discombobulated. She was always so calm at work and it gave me a small sense of relief to see that she was as off-kilter as I was.

"We um, that is, Nate and I are having regular meetings with the planner, and everything is on track for the party in two weeks. The RSVPs are mostly in, and we have reconfirmed with catering to make sure everything is on plan. We've got a small team working on the decorating. It's all going to be beautiful. We're hoping it will be even better than last year."

James nodded approvingly. "What about the publicity side?" he asked.

"We are all set," I told James. "We've sent our reminder emails to anyone who has not RSVPed yet. We've been building some hype on social media. The photographers are all confirmed, and we will be live tweeting pictures from the actual event. We're setting up a Flickr folder and will be uploading all the pictures there for other purposes. People will be asked to sign a media release as they check in."

James nodded in satisfaction, looking from me to Holly. "Good job you two. You really seem to be a great....team."

Maybe it was my imagination but there seemed to be a bit of innuendo there. Holly's eyes shot to me, looking vaguely alarmed, then quickly returned to looking towards James. Her hands were gripping the table so hard I could see her knuckles turn white from across the table.

I saw Lana smile knowingly at me from her place next to Holly, telling me that we had been a bit obvious and she was happy about it. Holly might not think we were a good match, but her friends did, so at least that was something.

Holly

It had been a couple of weeks since that scene in Nate's office and we had settled into a comfortable routine. He was still flirty with me, but he wasn't coming on so strong. Somehow that made me more obsessed with him. It was embarrassing really. Here I was a 45-year-old woman and I was breathlessly waiting to see him every morning when he brought me my morning chai. Whenever I ran into him out in the office somewhere I would feel giddy, despite giving myself a stern talking to every time. I found myself looking up every time someone walked by my office door, wondering if it was him.

After the meeting where he caught us staring at each other James came to my office to tease me about Nate. Honestly, sometimes he was like a gossipy old woman. He loved to know everything that was going on with his employees.

"What's with you and the kid in marketing?" James had asked me as he flopped into a guest chair and put his feet up on my desk, settling in for a chat.

I looked at him curiously. He was with Nina now, but I wondered why we had never felt attracted to each other. Maybe we knew each other too well; our years of friendship had left us completely comfortable in each other's presence. He had always felt more like a brother than a friend or a boss.

"Nothing," I said too quickly. I could feel a flush rising onto my face. James quirked an eyebrow, calling me on my bullshit. "He's just a flirty guy," I rushed to continue.

"Please," James said. "It's me. I see how you two look at each other. You get totally flustered whenever he's around and you would have to be blind not to notice the heat between you two."

I shook my head but before I could respond he added, "I hear there's an office pool betting on how long until you two get together."

"What?!?!" I shrieked, my eyes widened in alarm. "Oh my god, are you kidding?"

He shook his head and smiled. "I've got twenty bucks on a week from Saturday."

"That Saturday is the client party," I reminded him.

"I know. I'm betting the relief of the party being over with, coupled with alcohol, will loosen you up enough to take a chance on someone who is clearly head over heels for you."

"James!" I laughed. "You said it yourself, he's a kid."

"I was only teasing you, Hol," he said. "He's what, six years younger? That's not a big deal."

I leaned back in my chair and sighed deeply. "Try nine. He's only 36. Way too young for me."

"Oh, so you have been thinking about it," James said triumphantly.

"I'm not going to date someone so much younger," I told him. "He's just playing, there's no way he's really interested in someone like me."

James sat up and looked at me with a serious expression on his face. "Look Holly, you know I want what's best for you, always. You're a beautiful and accomplished woman who deserves love," he said. "It's obvious something is there between you two. I have never seen you so distracted by someone. So he's a bit younger, so what? You know as well as I do that some of the best relationships are based on differences. Including mine."

He stood up and started towards the door. "Give the kid a chance, Hol, that's all I'm saying. He seems like a good guy." He paused in the doorway and gave me a mischievous grin. "Besides, I think you make a good cougar."

I picked up my rubber stress ball and threw it at him as he ducked out the door, laughing. But I thought about what he said for the rest of the day. His words played on a non-stop loop in my brain.

The morning of the client party finally came, and I was up before dawn, amped up. I arrived at the venue early, eager to get a start on the decorations. I was standing on a step ladder, reaching to hang something on the wall, when I heard a low whistle.

"Holy crap," Nate's voice came from behind me. I started, then looked over my shoulder to see his gaze firmly focused on my ass.

"What?" I said self-consciously. I was wearing leggings and a t-shirt, and my shirt had pulled up above my waistband as I reached, offering him a perfect view of my chunky middle-aged ass. I stood awkwardly on the ladder, my face burning, while he continued to stare at my butt as if he had never seen one before. I cleared my throat and he seemed to drag his eyes away, up to my face.

"I would like to take this moment to thank whoever invented leggings," he said huskily. "That view is incredible." His eyes were dark and burning in his face and when I lowered my own gaze, I noticed a distinct bulge in his jeans. A sizable one.

Hmm, I guess I look better in these leggings than I thought.

Flummoxed, I started down the ladder, but I was distracted and just missed the bottom rung. I cried out, thinking I would fall, but Nate jumped forward and grabbed my waist, easing my feet slowly towards the floor as if I weighed nothing. I shivered at the feeling of his large hands gripping my hips.

I heard him take a deep breath before he dropped his hands. I turned around to thank him and realized he hadn't moved back, so we were standing only an inch or two apart. I looked up and gave him a shaky smile. "Thanks for saving me. It would be a bad day to get a concussion."

"I'll save you any time, baby," he answered, his voice deep with promise as he smiled down at me.

I rolled my eyes and stepped around him. "Let's get to work Gilbert."

We spent the next couple of hours finalizing the decorations and going over instructions with the caterers. One of the things I had realized the last few weeks was that Nate and I actually got along quite well.

I really liked him as a person and was starting to think of him as a friend. We had a lot of similar interests, and when he wasn't outrageously flirting with me, the conversation flowed easily. It made the time go by quickly, especially since the other two people who were supposed to be helping us decorate had both had something come up last minute that kept them from helping.

"I think that's it," I told him as I set the final centerpiece on a table. I centered the vase full of brightly colored Christmas ornaments and stepped back with a smile.

Nate turned slowly in a circle, eying the space critically. "It looks wonderful Holly," he said. "Classy yet festive. We did a great job."

"Yes we did," I agreed happily, walking towards him.

He reached out to shake my hand. "Teamwork!"

My smaller hand was engulfed in his larger hand as we shook, and neither of us let go. We stood there, hand in hand, while jolts of electricity moved up my arm and into my core. I could feel my breathing pick up and I inhaled deeply, trying to settle myself. I got a whiff of Nate and that just made it worse. For someone who had been laboring for several hours, he smelled damn good. I wasn't sure how, I knew I was probably all pitted out by now.

Glancing down, I could see my nipples poking eagerly through my shirt and my bra, clearly trying to get Nate's attention. No doubt my panties were wet as well.

I felt Nate's eyes on me and looked up, getting lost in the depth of his burning gaze. I felt myself start to sway closer to him. He stepped closer, stopping about an inch away, but he didn't make a move, waiting patiently. His words came back to me then: "When we do kiss, it will be because you initiate it."

The memory was like a jolt of cold water and I leapt back, removing my hand from his. I wrapped my arms nervously around myself as I backed away. "Well, um, I'm going to go home and relax for a few hours before the big event."

He quirked an eyebrow at me, looking amused, as I continued, "Thanks for your help, Gilbert. See you tonight!"

Nate

I loosened my tie as I looked around the enormous ballroom. The party was finally breaking up, and it had been an unqualified success. All of our visiting customers seemed to have a great time, and our live tweeting had garnered lots of attention on social media, both from those in attendance and those who hadn't made it. James seemed thrilled.

I looked across the room, my eyes locking on to Holly automatically as they did every time she was in the vicinity. She had kicked off her high heels and was slouching in a chair at a far table, chatting with James, his fiancée Nina, Lana, and Ian. Holly looked tired but satisfied.

She was so beautiful it took my breath away. All night I had watched her work the room, elegant in her fancy black dress, her hair coiled in a sophisticated bun at the nape of her neck, although several wild tendrils had escaped as the night wore on.

Holly was skilled at small talk and seemed to have a knack for finding people who were alone and chatting them up before introducing them to someone else. The perfect hostess.

That moment we had earlier, when I was sure she was finally going to kiss me, kept flashing through my mind all night. I wasn't sure what had stopped her, but suddenly I was tired of waiting for her. I was afraid she would never move things along for us.

Drawn by instinct, I headed in her direction but was waylaid by Jessica. She stepped in front of me, sliding her hand up my chest and smiling up at me seductively.

"Great party, huh?" she said. Her eyes were a little bright, like she had indulged in some of the free drinks at the party. I wondered idly if the party planner was supposed to drink on the job.

"Yes, it was. Thanks for your help Jessica," I said neutrally. "Great job."

I started to step around her, but she slid her other hand down my arm and grabbed my hand, her other hand still resting familiarly on my chest. She was an attractive woman, but I felt absolutely nothing when she touched me. It was like my body only wanted Holly.

"How about we celebrate with a night cap?" she asked huskily, her intent clear. "I don't live too far from here."

The hair on the back of my neck prickled, and I looked up to see Holly glaring in our direction, watching us carefully. Was she jealous? That would be favorable development. I had picked up on her irritation with Jessica's flirting more than once when we were meeting.

As gently as possible I disengaged from Jessica and took a step back. "Thanks Jessica, you're a great girl, but I'm kind of hung up on someone else right now."

She followed my gaze to Holly, who was still watching us with a pissed off look on her face.

"Holly?" Jessica asked me incredulously. "She's kind of old for you, isn't she? She must be close to 50." The planner's face twisted with her mean-spirited words. "You need to date someone your own age."

"No thanks," I said firmly, stepping around her. I could feel her shocked gaze on my back as I made my way to Holly. I stalked towards her, each step full of intent, my eyes on her. The rest of the room faded into the background around me as I focused on her. She looked slightly alarmed, as if she could read my intent.

"Holly," I said when I finally reached her. "Can I talk to you? Alone?"

"I'm relaxing right now," she said, sitting up primly in her chair but looked visibly nervous. "Can it wait until Monday?"

Out of the corner of his eye I could see the other two couples watching the action with interest.

"It really can't wait," I said firmly, making my voice deep and authoritative. "Come with me."

Her eyes widened with excitement, something I filed away for later. I grabbed her hand and pulled her to her feet, and she let out a surprised squeak. I turned and headed towards the door, leading Holly along as she protested, "Wait, my shoes!"

I thought I heard James say, "Whoo-hoo, I won the pool!" as I pulled Holly away.

I walked down the hall to an empty meeting room that I had spotted earlier. I pulled Holly into the room and closed the door behind us, pressing the lock. The room was dim, lit only by the moon and the ambient light from the city outside the windows.

"What the hell are you doing Nate?" she asked, pulling her hand away as soon we entered the room.

I leaned against the door, crossing my ankles and forcing myself to look casual despite the anxiety coursing through my veins. I hoped I was doing the right thing.

"How long are you going to make me wait Holly?" I asked.

She cocked her head to the side, her brow creasing with confusion. "Wait? For what?"

"For you to kiss me," I answered with forced patience. "I know I said I would wait for you to make the next move Holly, but you're killing me here. I think we've had the longest foreplay in the history of foreplay. It's time to move onto the kissing."

I heard her give a little gasp as she brought up her outrage. "I am not going to kiss you," she said in irritation. "I told you that. More than once."

"Scared?" I taunted her.

"Why would I be scared?" she asked.

"Because you know once you kiss me, you'll have to admit that you like me." I smirked at her and she glared back. "Once you get a taste of this," I gestured towards my mouth, "you won't be able to get enough of me."

"I can't believe your ego, Gilbert," she said. "I can guarantee you that would not happen."

"Prove it," I said, hoping I wasn't pushing her too far. "I dare you."

"All right, you know what, fine!" she said hotly, glaring at me. "If that's what it will take, I will kiss you. Once. Then you will promise that you'll back the fuck off and quit flirting with me."

"I'll back off if you can honestly tell me you feel nothing when we kiss," I countered.

"Fine, if that's what it will take to make you leave me alone, I'll do it," she said stubbornly. She stalked over to stand in front of me where I was leaning against the door. "Keep your hands on the door," she instructed.

I leaned forward obligingly, keeping my hands pressed to the door on my sides. She stepped closer and reached up, grasping my head, and pulling me down to her. She hesitated only a moment, meeting my eyes, before pressing her lips against mine.

The instant her lips touched mine I knew for sure that my instincts had been right all along. If I had any doubts that she was the one for me, I let them go right then. Her lips were soft and sweet, and her touch was like coming home. A sense of rightness settled over me.

She pressed her lips against mine for a long moment, tasting me gently, then nipped my lower lip. I obliged by opening my mouth. She pressed her curvy body against mine, deepening the kiss, exploring my mouth with her tongue. She tasted like wine and chocolate and something uniquely Holly. I knew I could die right now and leave this world a happy man.

She broke the kiss with a gasp, taking a half a step back, staring at me, her eyes wide with shock. We looked at each other for a long moment before she lunged back towards me. I lifted my hands from the door, catching her and pulling her close to my quickly growing erection. I took control of the kiss, angling her head and plundering the sweetness of her mouth.

Holly dropped her hands to my butt, squeezing me tight and pulling me even closer to her. I could feel her soft plump breasts pressing into my chest. I slipped my fingers into her hair, angling her head so I could kiss her deeper, and felt the silky strands release from whatever was holding it into the fancy bun at the nape of her neck.

I walked her backwards a few feet, still kissing her, until Holly's legs met the conference table. Without breaking the kiss, I lifted her onto the table, moving between her knees to align our bodies closer. She reached down and shoved her skirt up a few more inches towards her hips, allowing her legs to widen more. I pressed my cock firmly against her core, feeling the heat of her through the layers of her panties and my clothing. Holly tilted her pelvis against me, heightening my excitement even more.

My hand slid down to palm her breast, rubbing around the nipple until I felt it harden under my fingers. I pinched it firmly and she moaned in my mouth, thrusting her pelvis against my cock again and again like she was trying to get herself off by friction alone. Her hands slid up under my suit jacket and clutched my shoulders, her nails biting against me through the fabric.

I was so hard I was worried I would come in my pants like I was fifteen again.

I moved my mouth away, kissing down her jaw and down her neck, before biting down firmly the sensitive spot where her neck met her shoulder. The desire to mark her as mine was coursing through my veins like a moral imperative. She gasped. "Oh my god, Nate!"

I straightened, pulling back slightly so I could look into her eyes. "Holly, you're so freaking hot," I ground out, my voice sounding like gravel. "I've wanted to do this since the minute I first laid eyes on you in that stupid Monday morning meeting. I knew it would be like this."

I dropped my hands to her thighs, stroking them gently as we both caught our breath. My heart was racing so fast I was afraid I might pass out. I stared into her eyes, seeing the answering passion and wonder there. I moved one hand up higher on her thigh, higher still, until my fingers met the crotch of her panties.

I smiled at her, as I stroked my finger back and forth along the fabric. "You're soaked for me Holly," I said softly, feeling unaccountably proud. "I guess you felt something when you kissed me after all."

Her eyes flared in annoyance, but then she seemed to come to a decision. "Did you lock the door when we came in?" she asked.

I nodded.

"Do you have a condom?" she continued.

I nodded again. "A gentleman is always prepared."

"Then shut the hell up and fuck me, Gilbert."

Holly

Nate's eyes widened in shock.

I knew the feeling, I was shocked myself. Shocked at how good it felt to kiss him, how right it felt. Shocked at how Nate's magic lips had brought me so close to orgasm without any clitoral stimulation. I always needed some clit action to get off. Shocked at how I had just demanded he fuck me, right here, right now, on a conference table in a hotel with our boss a few rooms away. The idea that we might get caught only heightened my excitement.

None of this behavior was like me, even when I was younger, and while I knew I wasn't acting like my normal self, right now I didn't care. I only knew I would die if Nate wasn't inside me soon.

"Wait. How much have you had to drink, Holly?" he asked me, his voice shaky.

I sighed impatiently. "Enough to feel good but not enough to be drunk. Why? Are you drunk?"

He smiled and shook his head. "Only on you."

I leaned forward and unzipped his pants as he gasped. I slipped my hands underneath his briefs and pulled his straining erection free, rubbing my finger against the pre-cum dripping from the tip. Holy hell he was huge. It had been a while since I had been with anyone, I only hoped everything was still stretchy down there.

He put one hand on top of mine, stilling the movement of my hands. "Are you sure Holly?" he asked sweetly. I could tell he was grasping to maintain his control. "We can wait if you aren't ready to take this step."

We both groaned as I started working my hand up and down his firm length without any conscious direction from my brain. He was long and wide and felt incredible in my hands. "No waiting," I gasped. "I need you inside me. Now."

Nate pulled his wallet from his pants and took out a condom, ripping it open with his teeth. I took it from him and slowly smoothed it down his penis. He leaned forward and kissed me deeply while I continued to stroke his cock, feeling it grow impossibly larger with my touch.

When we came up for air, he grabbed my hips and pulled me closer to the edge of the table. I leaned back onto my elbows, wrapping my legs around his hips. He pushed my panties aside, dipping his fingers into the warmth of my pussy. He slid his fingers up and down my slit a few times, humming happily. His fingertips grazed my clit and I damn near levitated off the table.

"Now Nate, now," I gasped. "Please!"

He lined his cock up with my opening. Our eyes met in the dim light as he slowly pushed his way into me. I gasped at the feeling of fullness, taking a deep breath to help my internal muscles relax. When he was fully seated inside me he paused, looking at me with such adoration I felt tears threaten.

"Holly, you feel so good," he whispered reverently, moving one hand to brush a stray lock of hair behind my ear. I pressed my cheek into his hand as he continued, "Better than I even dreamed about. I want to make this good for you, but I don't know how long I'm going to last."

I thrust my hips up against him, settling him even deeper and drawing a groan from both of us. "Quick now, slow later," I grunted. "I really need you to start moving Nate. Now."

His eyes flared. "I love it when you get bossy," he said with a sinful smile.

He started pounding into me as he leaned over me on the table, keeping his weight off me by propping himself up on his hands. His pubic bone rubbed against my clit with every stroke. The force of his thrusts made me slide up the table a little bit with every push. He found my hands, intertwining our fingers and pressing them against the table on either side of my waist for leverage to keep me in place.

My nipples tightened painfully, the movement of our bodies causing the fabric of my bra to shift over the tips just enough to heighten my excitement. My entire body felt like it was on fire, like I was burning up from the inside out.

I looked up at Nate's figure looming over me and smiled. We were both fully clothed, having a quickie on a table in a conference room, and it was hands down the single hottest moment of my life. I had never felt so out of control, so desperate for someone.

I could feel my body tightening as it chased orgasm, impossibly fast. Weeks of flirting with Nate was all the foreplay I needed.

"I'm getting close Nate," I wailed. "Don't hold back, give me it all."

He adjusted his position so he could hold my hips tightly and tilt them up more, getting even deeper inside me. From this angle he was hitting the bundle of nerves inside me that set me off like a rocket in just a few more hard strokes.

"Oh my god!" I cried out loudly. "Nate. Nate."

I felt my entire body tighten up as my orgasm hit me, then I started shaking as wave after wave of pleasure rolling through my body. Nate continued to pound into me while I chanted his name over and over again like a prayer.

"Holly," he groaned. "You feel so good. I'm coming, baby." I heard him grunt deeply a second before he stiffened, and suddenly I felt his warm seed pouring into the condom. "Holly!"

I was still coming down from my own orgasm when he collapsed on top of me, smashing me between his hard body and the table, and resting his face on my breasts. Our breathing was loud in the silence of the room; we were both panting like we had sprinted a mile with Usain Bolt.

I realized I was coated in a sheen of sweat. The room felt warm and the smell of sex hung in the air. I was sure my make-up was sliding off my sweaty face and I silently thanked the gods of sex that the light was dim.

Nate finally lifted his weight off me and rose onto his elbows, leaning down to meet my eyes before pressing a soft kiss on my lips. "That was fucking incredible," he said, his gaze so tender and loving that it melted something deep in my heart.

I nodded, smiling like a loon. "It sure was."

"I can't believe you made us wait so long to do that," he said with a teasing smile. "We've really been missing out on some fun."

I smacked his shoulder. "OK Gilbert, get off me so we can check on the situation in the ballroom and get the hell out of here so we can do that again." I paused, briefly insecure. "You want to do it again, right?"

He stood back up, pulling me to a seated position as he slid out of my body. "Are you fucking kidding me right now woman? I'm already getting hard for you again and I haven't even taken the condom off yet," he said.

I looked down at his penis, and sure enough it was starting to harden again. "Wow, you're going to be ready to go again so soon?" I asked, a touch of awe in my voice.

He nodded, giving me a sexy smile, then leaned forward to give me one last quick chaste kiss on the lips.

"Well I guess I finally see the benefit of dating a younger man," I drawled as I stood up and adjusted my dress. "Let's figure out whose house is closest and get the hell out of here."

Nate

I awoke with a start, my arm tingling. I heard a soft snore and looked down, smiling when I saw Holly sleeping on my arm. Her hair was spread out in a riot of messy curls, her face relaxed in sleep. I took a deep breath and sent a quick prayer up to whatever gods existed that Holly wouldn't wake up and change her mind about us.

We had rushed back to her place last night after we left the hotel, likely breaking several traffic laws in our rush to get some place where we could be alone. Fortunately, she owned a place downtown so we didn't have far to go.

After making out like teenagers in the elevator we had practically fallen in the door of her condo. Despite our vow to go slower the second time, I had her bent over the nearby dining room table with her dress up around her waist within thirty seconds of opening the door. With my hand wrapped around that beautiful hair I had taken her from behind, playfully tapping the generous curve of her ass with my other hand while she swore colorfully in both English and Spanish.

We both needed some recovery time after that. We snuggled together on the couch, snacking and sharing a bottle of wine while we talked. I knew she was concerned about our age difference, but the truth was none of that mattered to me. We were well matched. I loved talking to her. I loved kissing her. I loved...well, it was much too early to be talking like that.

Eventually we wound up in her bed where I went down on her and made her orgasm twice – once with my fingers and once with my tongue. When I finally took her for the third time, we stared intimately into each other's eyes the whole time as I slid slowly in and out of her body. There was no doubt in my mind we were not just having sex, we were making love. No sexual experience I had ever had in my life had been that intimate.

We had both passed out from exhaustion soon after that.

I looked around Holly's bedroom curiously, noting the warm colors and comfortable furniture. Based on the light coming through the windows, it had to be late morning. Normally I wasn't one for sleeping in, but after working on the party all day and making love to Holly all night, I needed my rest. Despite what Holly thought, 36 wasn't really that young, and I needed my recovery time.

I felt Holly start to waken and smiled at her momentary confusion as she rubbed her hand down my chest. I saw the instant she remembered what happened, her eyes opening wide.

I leaned down and pressed a soft kiss on the top of her head. "Good morning sunshine," I said, my voice rough with sleep.

She blinked a few times. "Good morning Gilbert," she croaked. She cleared her throat. "You're still here?"

"Where else would I be?" I asked, rubbing my hand up and down her bare arm.

She shook her head. "Hold that thought, I really need to pee," she said, pushing herself off the bed. I smiled appreciatively as I watched her rush naked into the adjacent bathroom. She returned a few minutes later, a robe tied around that curvy little body, her hair damp at the temples like she had washed her face while she was in there.

She looked at me lounging on the bed, her face uncertain. "Um, would you like some breakfast or something?" she asked. Her gaze landed on the phone she had plugged in near the bed, and her eyes widened. "Holy crap! It's after 9:00! I never sleep this late."

I stood up and stalked over towards her, buck naked, noting her appreciative gaze on my chest. I leaned in for a chaste kiss. "Me neither, but someone wore me out last night. I would love breakfast. And a quick shower, if you don't mind."

She nodded towards the bathroom. "There are towels in the cabinet behind the door."

"You could join me," I offered suggestively, even while I instinctively knew she needed her space right now. I could see the confusion and fear written all over her face.

"You shower, I'll cook," she said firmly. "I could eat my own arm I'm so hungry."

I took my time in the shower, giving her some time to process, then met her in the kitchen dressed in last night's pants and my undershirt. Her eyes tracked my biceps and I tried not to preen. I wasn't in my 20s anymore, but I worked hard to stay in shape.

I looked around, actually noticing her place for the first time. It was clearly expensive, a downtown condo with a doorman, a view of the city, and high-end appliances. "Nice place," I said. "James must be paying you well."

She blushed slightly. "Thanks, but I bought this place when I worked in tech. I was making crazy money then and working so many hours I didn't have time to spend a dime. Then when they laid me off, I sold all my stock in the company and used the proceeds to pay off my mortgage and my car."

I raised my eyebrows and whistled. "Wow, impressive."

"It all worked out for the best. Their stock tanked about six months later, so it would have been mostly worthless if I had waited. And I went into my unemployment debt free, which gave me more options. When James offered me a low stress job, I was free to take it, even though the pay was much lower."

I leaned forward and gave her a quick kiss on the lips. "Beautiful and smart," I murmured.

She looked embarrassed. "Breakfast is ready," she said, clearing her throat. We sat side by side at the kitchen island, silently eating the scrambled eggs and bacon Holly had cooked. I heard Holly laugh softly and I looked at her curiously.

"I was just thinking that it only took us three tries before we actually had sex with our clothes off," she laughed.

I smiled and met her eyes as I bit into a slice of crispy bacon. "How about we try that again after breakfast, just to make sure we got the hang of it?" I suggested. "Practice makes perfect."

She smiled again and my breath caught in my throat. "OK Gilbert, you're on."

***

The next three weeks passed quickly. Holly and I were together every night, usually at her place, venturing out for long walks and dinners together. We kept our distance at work, although I still brought her a chai every morning.

Holly felt strongly about keeping our relationship a secret from our coworkers and I didn't have the heart to tell her that everyone had already figured out what was going on. I didn't want to freak her out, but apparently, we weren't as stealthy as we thought we were. Plus, James kept bragging about winning the "Holly and Nate Dating Pool".

No one seemed to have a problem with it, but I knew she needed more time to adjust to our new relationship. I was also well aware of the double standard in place for women who dated coworkers, and I didn't want to do anything to undermine her credibility at the company.

It was a couple days before Christmas and we were snuggling on the couch, drinking wine, and watching an old black and white holiday movie, when it all fell apart.

"Christmas is only a couple of days away," I pointed out. "What do you usually do for Christmas?"

Holly turned her head and looked up at me. "I usually go to my sister's house. She lives out in the far suburbs. My mom and my younger sister and I go there early on Christmas Eve to make tamales, then I stay over at one of their houses. They all live close to each other."

"Tamales?" I asked.

I must have looked confused because she added, "My mom is Mexican, so we make tamales for Christmas, it's a tradition in our culture. They take a long time to make though, and it's a lot of work, so we do it together."

"That sounds nice," I said. "Do you have a big family?" I asked, suddenly realizing that we hadn't talked about our families that much. Or at all.

She nodded. "Yeah, lots of cousins, nieces and nephews. It's usually a crowd. How about you, what do you do?"

"We all go to my parents on Christmas morning and spend the day together. My siblings are all married so they spend Christmas Eve with their in-laws."

Holly nodded, her gaze drifting back to the movie. "Cool."

"How about if we spend Christmas Eve with your family and Christmas Day with mine?" I suggested.

Holly stiffened next to me. "What are you talking about?"

I looked down at her, confused. "Huh?"

"We're not spending Christmas with each other's families Gilbert," she said firmly.

I frowned. "Why not. We're together now. We should meet each other's families. I know it's a little soon, but we'll have to meet them eventually. Might as well do it while everyone is together."

She was shaking her head before I even finished my sentence. "We have been dating for like three weeks, that's definitely not 'meet the family' point yet," she said. "Besides, it's not like this is ever going to be serious."

Her words hit me like a punch to the stomach. "This isn't serious?" I asked incredulously. "How can you say that? I thought we were on the same page now. Nothing about this feels casual."

Holly pushed away from me, leaning over to reach the remote and turn off the TV.

"Look Nate, this has been super fun. I love spending time with you and of course the sex is phenomenal," she said slowly, as if she were speaking to an exceptionally difficult child. "But we will never be anything more than casual. I thought you understood that."

"Based on what?" I asked.

"I wasn't aware that I needed to spell it out for you," she said sharply. "I thought we both understood that this was just for fun."

"I'm not looking for fun Holly," I told her. "I'm looking for forever."

Her eyes widened. "I'm sure you believe that, but in time this will burn out and you'll find someone your own age, someone you have more in common with. Someone who can give you kids."

"Kids?" I said incredulously. "Who said anything about kids? And I think we have a lot in common."

"You know I'm 45 right?" she reminded me, her voice high and tight. "I'm too old to have kids. And I'm sure as hell too old to hold the attention of someone your age for more than a fling. I'm not going to be humiliated in front of your family and mine as the pathetic older woman playing around with a child."

I stood up abruptly, the anger and hurt coursing through my body like a wave. "Oh my god, again with this bullshit about age?" I said angrily. "I thought we were past that Holly. I'm a grown man damn it, I don't need you telling me what I want or what I feel. I have been crystal clear about this from day one: I want you. Not kids. Not someone younger. Just you."

She shook her head. "Nate..."

"No," I interrupted her. "I'm in love with you Holly. I think I have been in love with you since the day I met you. Doesn't that mean anything to you?"

Her eyes filled with tears and she reached her hands out to me before dropping them again. She opened her mouth and closed it again without speaking.

"I think you're in love with me too, even if you won't admit it," I continued. She gasped.

"There's no way in hell this feels like some casual fling to you. If you could just get past your stubborn preconceived notions about age and what I want and what people think, you would realize that something like this, what we have, doesn't just come along every day. It's real."

Tears were coursing down her face now. She pulled her knees up to her chest protectively. "No," she whispered. "I can't do this, Nate, it hurts too much, and it will just hurt that much more the longer we go on pretending that this can be something."

Her face looked grief stricken and it took everything in me not to take her in my arms and comfort her even while she was ripping my heart out of my chest with her words. "Someday you'll realize that I was right Nate, and us being together was a mistake. Then you'll leave me to find someone more suitable for you."

I moved towards the door, grabbing my jacket off the coat rack with such force it toppled over. I stopped and looked back at her. "Someday you'll realize you had a chance at a great love, the kind you dream about, and you threw it all away for no reason other than you're a coward."

I heard her sob loudly as I walked out the door.

Holly

"What the hell happened to you?"

My sister Adelaide was characteristically blunt as she opened her front door. "You look like crap," she added, taking my coat.

"Gee thanks, sis," I responded sadly.

I had gone through the last few days in a haze of grief. I had been like a reclusive zombie at work, going through the motions, hiding in my office, staring into space for long periods of time, totally useless. I couldn't even drag myself downstairs to get my morning chai, because just thinking about how Nate brought me a chai every single day for months made me want to cry.

I missed him bringing me chai. I missed him holding me while I slept. I missed him making me laugh. I just missed him. I knew that Nate wasn't faring much better when James came into my office the last day of work before the Christmas break, a concerned look on his handsome face.

"I've been waiting for you to talk to me," he announced as he once again put his feet on my desk. "We have always talked about everything. But clearly you need a push. What's going on?"

I had looked up at him with bleary eyes that I knew from the mirror were red and puffy from crying and sleeplessness. "Nate and I broke up," I shared, my voice shaky.

He waved his hand. "Yeah, yeah, everyone in the building figured that out from the way you two both look like angsty teenagers in a vampire movie," he said impatiently. "But what I don't get, is why? You seemed great together. You have great chemistry. He obviously is quite taken with you and I thought you really liked him too."

"He was getting too serious," I told him sadly. "He wanted us to spend Christmas together. Meet each other's families."

"The bastard!" James said wryly. "Why is that a problem, exactly?"

47

"You know this. He's too young for me. Eventually he would get tired of dating a middle-aged woman and then he would go find someone young and cute his own age. They would fall in love, get married and have beautiful babies." The words rushed out of me before I took a breath and added, "It's better to break up now before we're more invested and it hurts more than it does now."

"What the hell Holly?" he asked. "This isn't like you. You're 45 not 85. The guy is totally gone for you, anyone with eyes can see that."

I shrugged.

James continued. "Do you love him?"

I felt my eyes fill with tears and whispered, "Yes."

"Then nothing else matters. Love doesn't come around every day. So quit being an idiot."

He stood up as if the matter was closed and pointed at me with his boss face on. "You love him, he loves you, there's no reason not to be together. Especially when being apart makes you both so miserable. Go home early, no one's doing any work today anyway. Don't come back from break until you've figured this out."

I had spent the whole day yesterday rehashing James' words and moping around missing Nate, but I didn't know how to fix this. I knew I had hurt him, he had looked devastated when he left my apartment. I wondered if he had already moved on. Maybe he was taking Jessica to his family dinner for Christmas.

My sister's sharp tone pulled me out of my reverie. "Holly, did you hear me?" she asked. "Tell me what happened before Mom gets here."

I sat at my sister's kitchen island pouring out the whole story over a mimosa, amazingly dry-eyed. Maybe I was finally cried out.

Adelaide lifted her gaze from the chicken she was shredding and pointed the knife at me. "You are an idiot," she said.

My eyes widened with surprise. "What? You think I should stay with some young kid?" I asked.

"No, I think you should stay with the grown-ass adult man who is old enough to know his own mind and for some strange reason, despite all your weirdness and walls, decided that you are the woman for him."

She paused and looked at me carefully. "I think you should stay with the man you love and let everything else work itself out."

I did my best to put Nate out of my mind the next two days and be present with my family at Christmas. My sister's house was filled with family and friends and the two days passed quickly in a blur of food and games and alcohol. I could tell my mother was dying to interrogate me about my less than festive mood, but Adelaide must have talked her out of it because other than long speculative looks in my direction, she avoided asking me anything about my personal life.

When I got back to my place the day after Christmas, I was exhausted. I slept for three days straight and during the few hours I was actually awake, my mind kept going back to my conversations with James and Adelaide. I rehashed every conversation I had ever had with Nate, analyzing it from every angle.

What if he was serious? What if he really loved me, despite my age, despite my quirks, despite his other options? Could I trust that? Because as much as this hurt now, I knew if we spent more time together and he came to his senses farther down the road, it would be even more devastating for me.

Maybe Nate and my sister were both right, maybe I was a coward.

I thought long and hard about my life before Nate, and what it was like living without him now that I knew what I was missing. And finally, like a bolt of lightning it hit me: I had to get him back. I loved him too much to let him go.

Nate

My buddies and I had a tradition of meeting on New Year's Eve for a long hard game of basketball in the park. It was a brutal game, lots of pushing and elbows and sweaty exertion, and although we were all older now, we still played like a bunch of stupid teens. The last few years however, the injuries hurt more, and the recovery took a lot longer.

I was limping up the street to my townhouse when I saw a lone figure sitting on my stairs. I caught my breath. Holly. My heart started thudding rapidly and I suddenly felt lighter than I had in days. She had come back to me. Or at least I hoped that's why she was there.

She looked up cautiously as I walked towards her, then her expression changed to alarm. "Oh my god, Nate, what happened?" she asked. "Why are you limping like that?"

"Basketball accident," I said casually as I examined her face for a hint of why she was here. I drank in the sight of her like a thirsty man coming out of the desert. "Someone stepped on my knee. I'll be fine after I put some ice on it."

Her brow crinkled in confusion as she tried to work out how someone could step on my knee. But I wasn't interested in talking about my knee right now.

"Why are you here, Holly?" I asked. Even though my heart was singing with joy to see her again, I was cautious. She had really hurt me.

"Can I come in for a few minutes?" she asked softly, her face giving nothing away. I nodded and unlocked the door, gesturing for her to go in ahead of me. I limped to the kitchen and grabbed a beer, silently offering her one. She shook her head. I leaned against the counter and raised my eyebrows expectantly as I took a long pull from the bottle.

She cleared her throat nervously, then reached into her pocket, pulling out a piece of paper that was neatly folded in fourths. "It's New Year's Eve," she began.

"I know."

She met my eyes for a moment, then straightened her spine with resolve. I noted the dark circles under her eyes, like she hadn't been sleeping. I knew the feeling. Every night alone in my bed was torture without the woman I loved snuggling next to me, snoring in that adorable way she had.

"I like to make resolutions on New Year's Eve," she continued.

"Most people do," I answered, keeping my tone bored and uninterested.

I knew she was trying, but that didn't mean I had to make it easy for her. Her eyes flashed briefly with annoyance. There she was, the spirited woman I loved. Her voice was firmer now. "I want to share my resolutions with you."

I frowned. Resolutions? Where was she going with this?

"Holly."

"Please," she said softly. I nodded. Like I could deny her anything.

"Resolution one," she began. "Be more trusting."

She looked up at me, her eyes wide and searching. I nodded encouragingly as she took a deep breath.

"Resolution two, tell Nate I'm in love with him."

My heart sped up and I gripped my hands around the edge of the counter I leaned against. Were my ears deceiving me?

"Resolution three, beg Nate to take me back and give me another chance to get this right."

She stopped and slid the paper back into her coat pocket, her eyes on her feet.

"That's it?" I said with a teasing smile. "Only three resolutions?" I was cracking up inside that she had written those three down like she needed help to remember them.

She looked up and smiled hopefully. "Well, they say you should pick resolutions that are realistic and doable," she explained. "I also like to knock out my resolutions as soon as possible so I can start my year with a win."

"Is that a fact?" I responded.

She nodded and moved closer to me, her gaze searching my face. "I love you Gilbert," she said. "I know it took me a while to realize it, but I do love you. And I trust you when you say you love me too. Also, I miss you and have been so incredibly miserable without you."

We stared at each other for a long time, hope blooming between us. Finally, she added, "So, um, can we start again?"

I shook my head and her face fell. "I don't want to start again," I told her. "I don't want to go back to me bringing you chai and you ignoring me. How about we just make a shared resolution to pick up where we left off when we broke up?"

She launched herself forward and I caught her in my arms, my lips meeting hers hungrily. We kissed like we had been separated for years instead of a just over a week. Our kiss was a mutual claiming, and a promise for the future.

When we finally broke apart for air, she smiled up at me and said, "I thought for sure you were going to make me beg."

I wrapped her long hair around my fist and drew her closer again, pressing my erection against the cradle of her hips while her eyes widened in excitement.

"Oh, I'm going to make you beg all right," I told her, my voice dark with promise. "But not for forgiveness. I'm going to make you beg for permission to come. That will be your punishment for hurting me. Today I'm in charge, beautiful."

She smiled happily. "Great. Will we actually get our clothes off this time?"

I turned her and boosted her up onto the kitchen island, pulling her jeans off while I laid her down like a buffet. "Maybe next time."

Epilogue - Holly

"Hurry up Gilbert, it's almost midnight. They're about the start the countdown," I called.

I looked up as my handsome husband came in, loaded down with a platter of snacks, two glasses and a bottle of champagne.

Our rescue dog Barney skittered out of the way as Nate strode over to the couch, depositing everything on the coffee table. He plopped down next to me and pulled me under his arm. I leaned against his chest, as I had so often before, feeling warm and content.

We watched the countdown on TV then kissed deeply. "Cheers to three great years together," Nate said, clinking his champagne glass against mine.

"And our fourth New Year's Eve together," I reminded him with an affectionate smile. I took a sip of champagne. "What's your New Year's resolution?" I asked him.

"To stay 39 forever," he said promptly.

Nate's 40th birthday was in January and he was uncharacteristically melancholy about it. "Hey," I protested. "I'm looking forward to you turning 40. We'll finally be in the same decade," I reminded him. "At least for a year."

"Yeah, but will you still love me when I'm some guy in his 40s instead of a hot young stud in his 30s?" he asked, wiggling his eyebrows at me.

I set my glass down and wrapped my arms around his neck, looking deep in his eyes. "Gilbert, you'll always be a hot young stud to me," I told him solemnly. "Even when you're a wrinkled up old man and I'm a wrinkled up old lady."

He smiled and leaned in to give me a deep kiss. Despite over three years together, I still felt a zing whenever he kissed me.

"Marrying you was the best decision I ever made, Holly" he told me. I smiled. "And you're the best resolution I ever made, Gilbert."

***

Did you like this book? Show the love and leave me a review. Reviews are like puppies, they make you feel happy. Be sure to Join my mailing list[1] to get a FREE BOOK and keep up to date on all the new releases and special sales.

---

1. https://storyoriginapp.com/giveaways/62ee758e-068f-11eb-904e-c373f6014fe1

Special Preview

Until You Came Along by Rose Bak

Jen heard the rumbling from all the way in the kitchen. Wiping her hands on a towel, she walked to the front porch to watch the two large buses drive up the long driveway to the farmhouse. Belching smoke, they idled and came to a stop, one behind the other.

Although it wasn't even 10 a.m. yet, the sun shone brightly in the summer sky, showcasing the dust left in the wake of the parked buses. A bird squawked loudly in the sudden silence as a serious looking young woman scurried out of the first bus, glasses askew, a clipboard gripped in one hand, cellphone in another. Two large mountains of men followed her, hulking shadows.

"Jen Oliver? The band is here. We'll just come in and...." she moved to enter the house, but Jen stood her ground, blocking the door.

"Where are they?" she asked the woman, her tone icy. "And who are you exactly?"

The woman looked flustered for a brief moment before her stern mask fell back down again. She shuffled her cell phone into the hand with the clipboard and stuck out her now-free hand to shake. "I'm Simone. I manage the band."

Jen ignored her hand. "Well, manage them out of those buses. They don't get to send the help out to greet their sister."

Simone looked confused as she dropped her hand back to her side. "They're all sleeping. They had a late night. We'll just come in and check...."

"Still up all night and sleeping all day, huh? That's been the same since they were teenagers." Jen shook her head. On the farm they had all been taught the value of hard work – up before dawn, work all day, and early to bed. Somehow those lessons hadn't really stuck with her brothers despite her grandparents' best efforts over the years.

Of course, the boys, as she still thought of them, had been away from the farm for ten years now, chasing fame and fortune as the biggest boy band to hit the charts since N Sync. Like the band that came before them, the Oliver Boys had grown up but continued to enchant teenage girls across the world with their pop tunes.

Simone clearly felt protective of the boys. "They played last night in Wichita you know," she said sternly. "The show went until almost midnight, then they met the fans and press for hours after."

"By meet the fans and press do you mean got drunk and partied?" Jen's tone did little to hide her opinion of the boys and their reputation for debauched partying.

Simone shook her head. "They've mostly settled down now. There's not as much partying as there used to be when they were younger. But they still need to make an effort to meet people, it's part of the job. Now we'll just come in and...."

Jen shook her head. "Well," she drawled. "When they wake up from their so-called job, you send them on in. The rest of you need to find some other place to bunk. I'm not running a hotel for drunken roadies here."

A slight movement behind Simone caught Jen's eyes. One of the giant men flanking Simone shook with repressed laughter, his mouth twisted in a smirk but his face otherwise impassive. Jen looked at him for the first time. He was the size of a small tank, several inches over 6 feet tall, with impossibly wide shoulders and large biceps. His hair was a dark blond, "dishwater blonde" her grandma would call it, worn military short. He was dressed all in black, and she noticed a gun on the shoulder holster. Jen wondered why he felt he needed a gun out here in the middle of nowhere. She felt him watching her and she raised her eyes to his, a shiver of awareness coursing through her, although she couldn't make out his eyes behind the dark sunglasses.

"Miss Oliver..." Simone started again.

"Jen"

"OK, then, Jen, we need to do a security sweep before the boys come in. If you could just move aside, we'll get started." Simone nodded decisively.

"A security—-what the hell are you talking about?"

Simone turned to the man who'd been staring at Jen earlier. "This is Nick, he's head of security for the band. He'll be doing a security sweep and assessment with Brian here," she pointed at the second silent man.

"We don't need a security sweep. This place is as safe as it comes. We don't even lock the doors in these parts."

Simone shook her head again, vibrating with irritation and clearly not used to people disobeying her orders. "No way. The boys don't go anywhere without a security check ahead of time. I'm afraid I have to insist."

Jen shot her a look filled with venom, her tone as cold as ice. "You can insist all you like but this is my property. You have no right to it, and neither do the boys. Y'all can just run along now, I'm not having some ginormous strangers poking around my property. Don't make me sic the dogs on you." Simone's mouth dropped open.

This was an empty threat. Jen's three dogs looked mean, but they were incurably friendly. They were just as likely to lick a person to death as bite them. Jen had a sneaking suspicion that if someone tried to kill her the dogs would jump over her body and leave with the killer. But these music people didn't need to know that. If there was one thing Jen hated, it was music people. They were way too self-important and proud.

"Excuse me ma'am," the guy called Nick interrupted.

"Jen," she repeated, a trace of irritation in her tone.

He inclined his head. "Sorry. Jen. As Simone mentioned, I'm head of security for the band. We've had some issues and I would be very appreciative if my team could just poke around for a bit and make sure there's nothing amiss." His tone was deferential and charming, which only heightened Jen's suspicions.

"What kind of issues?"

"I'm afraid I'm not at liberty to discuss that ma—I mean Jen."

"Then I'm afraid I'm not at liberty to grant you access to my property. You step foot off that driveway, and I'll shoot you myself, right after I set the dogs on you. And you," she pointed at Simone, "better make sure no one bothers me again until I see those boys on my porch." She spun on her heel and slammed the door. It was going to be a long day.

***

For more of Jen's story, check out Until You Came Along *by Rose Bak. Available at select online retailers.*

About the Author

Rose Bak has been obsessed with books since she got her first library card at age five. She is a passionate reader with an e-reader bursting with thousands of beloved books.

Although Rose enjoys writing both fiction and nonfiction, romance novels have always been her favorite guilty pleasure, both as a reader and an author. Rose's contemporary romance books focus on strong female characters over age 35 and the alpha males who love them. Expect a lot of steam, a little bit of snark, and a guaranteed happily ever after.

Rose lives in the Pacific Northwest with her family, and special needs dogs. In addition to writing, she also teaches accessible yoga and loves music. Sadly, she has absolutely no musical talent so she mostly sings in the shower.

Please sign up for Rose's newsletter[1] to get a free book and keep up to date on all the latest news.

---

1. *https://storyoriginapp.com/giveaways/62ee758e-068f-11eb-904e-c373f6014fe1*

Other Books by Rose Bak

The Diamond Bay Contemporary Romance Series
Brand New Penny
Fresh as a Daisy
Right as Rain
Bite-Sized Shifters Paranormal Romance Series
Wolf Doctor
Kat's Dog
Designer Wolf
The Good with Numbers Holiday Romance Series
Love Unmasked
The Thanksgiving Scrooge
Maid for Christmas
Countdown to Love
Valentine's Lottery
The Oliver Boys Band Contemporary Romance Series
Until You Came Along
Rock Star Teacher
Rock Star Writer
Rock Star Neighbor
Loving the Holidays Contemporary Romance Series
Dating Santa
New Year's Steve
Independence Dave
Beach Wedding
Together Again
Non-fiction
What to Do If You Find a Cougar in Your Living Room: Self-Care in an Uncaring World

Catch up with these and other stories coming soon. Join my newsletter for more information[1] or follow my author page on your favorite retailer.

COUNTDOWN TO LOVE

1.   *https://storyoriginapp.com/giveaways/62ee758e-068f-11eb-904e-c373f6014fe1*

Ingram Content Group UK Ltd.
Milton Keynes UK
UKHW010633050623
422889UK00001B/264

9 798201 309817